For Jesse Edwards — in time for
the next adventure, welcome! ~ J.L.

tiger tales
5 River Road, Suite 128, Wilton, CT 06897
Published in the United States 2019
Originally published in Great Britain 2019
by Little Tiger Press Ltd.
Text and illustrations copyright © 2019 Jonny Lambert
ISBN-13: 978-1-68010-152-2
ISBN-10: 1-68010-152-8
Printed in China
LTP/1400/2642/0219

For more insight and activities,
visit us at www.tigertalesbooks.com

LET'S ALL CREEP THROUGH CROCODILE CREEK

by Jonny Lambert

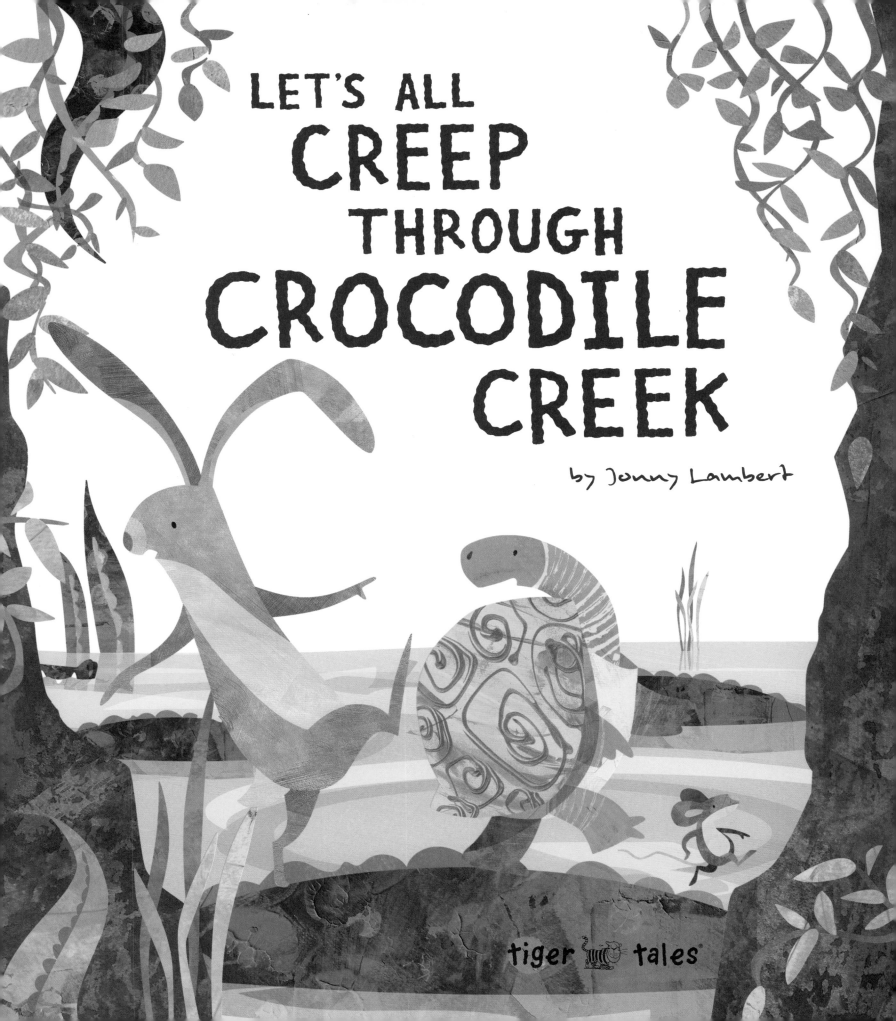

tiger tales

The sun sank slowly in the sky.
"We'd better get home before dark," said Mouse.
"Let's use the shortcut through the creek."

"Good question, Shelly," nodded Mouse
as they all set off together.

A crocodile has a knobby,
bumpy back.

And away they ran from the sneaky, snappy crocodiles.